T0129022

In My Minds Eye

BETTY BURDEN WOOD

authorHOUSE®

AuthorHouse™
1663 Liberty Drive
Bloomington, IN 47403
www.authorhouse.com
Phone: 1-800-839-8640

Published by AuthorHouse 2/29/2012

ISBN: 978-1-4634-4076-3 (sc)
ISBN: 978-1-4634-4074-9 (hc)
ISBN: 978-1-4634-4075-6 (e)

Library of Congress Control Number: 2011913114

This Book is to

Donald Rushing and his wife, Kathy Champagne Rushing of New Orleans, Louisiana, for being the most kind, sweetest and unselfish people they are. I love Donald and Kathy as if they were my own precious children.

Contents

The Mighty Polk County Storm 1

Returning The Money 11

Journey To The Graveyard 21

Kept Secret 29

Never Again 35

Vacation 39

Donalds Discovery 47

Going Back Home 53

The Scarlet Angel 57

Murder At Midnight 67

Gone Fishing 91

The Mighty Polk County Storm

THE MORRIS FAMILY had just finished eating their evening meal, when a mighty gust of wind and rain pounded on the windows and doors, causing all the curtains and papers and everything that was loose to fly around in the house.

"What in the world is that and what is going on?? Jean Morris asked her husband in a very shaky voice. Everyone was scared. "It must be a cyclone. Let's close all the windows and doors", her husband answered.

All the family rushed about trying to close the windows and doors, as rain came pouring down. The wind was so strong they could hardly close the doors. It kept pushing Phil Morris backward as the tried to shut the door. The strong wind was howling and the rain was so dense, they could hardly see the barn or the chicken house.

Phil Morris ushered his family away from the front window where they were watching the hypnotizing forces outside. They could hear trees falling and parts of the house roof flying around. It sounded like the roar of a freight train coming through. Only thing they could do now was huddle together and pray until it was all over and everything was calm again. It seemed as though time had stood still until the awful agonizing storm began to quite down a little.

Phil Morris opened the door to peep outside. "Get your slicker, Jess. We need to check on the stock. He grabbed his raincoat and hat from a nail by the door. He and his oldest son ran to the barn.

As the two hustled across the back yard, they saw

that trash and all kind of debris was scattered over the yard and the big black wash pot was full of water, leaves and branches. The ripe and bucket from the well were both gone, nowhere to be seen.

Jack, the family dog, had herded the mules and cows into the barn before the storm hit and then had taken shelter underneath the front porch to avoid the storm.

Night fall was rapidly approaching. The three Morris children were hurriedly running around gathering as much of what was left of their outdoor possessions as they could. Their father went in the house to get the milk bucket and rushed to the barn to milk the cow.

Jean Morris was busy in the kitchen, clearing the table, putting away the leftovers and getting the dishes ready to wash.

As she moved around the kitchen, she was humming Amazing Grace. It was an old song she, her mother and grandmother had hummed or sang while doing their housework.

"Guess I came from a ling line of hummers", she

thought to herself, feeling relieved and thankful the quick and furious storm had blown over and left them all safe.

Suddenly, Annie, the youngest of her children came running in the back door. "Ma, Ma, come quick! Look what we found in the front yard! Hurry, Ma, I think the storm blowed it in."

Jean Morris could not help but to laugh as she looked at her little girl. Her long red hair was rumpled and wet with sweat, and her big blue eyes shone with excitement as she urged her mother to hurry.

Jean grabbed a dish towel and dried her hands as she hurriedly walked through the house, behind the child that kept prodding her toward the front door.

"A new hatching of chicks or guineas", she thought. It didn't take much to excite Annie. The hens and guineas they owned had nests strewn all over the farm and many of them were full of eggs.

As she and Annie went through the front door, Jean saw her two sons and Jake the dog across the yard and near the road. As she made her way toward them, she marveled at the amount of limbs and leaves that covered the ground, making her aware of how strong the storm as been. Much of the split rail fence that had she separated the yard from the road was now lying flat along with their rusty old mailbox. Many of her flowers she had planted and pampered were on the ground and the blossoms were scattered across the yard. A lot of the trash and debris she couldn't recognize in the faltering evening light, but the light green shingles from the roof, she did.

"Phil will have to be on top of the house tomorrow", she thought to herself. "I hope it's not a hot day."

Annie's tight clutch on her hand urged her on as she looked again toward her two sons. They were crouching over what looked to be an old cotton sack and their youngest son, Luke, had his hand jammed inside. Just as Jean walked up behind him, he pulled his arm out and Jean wiped her eyes to believe what she was seeing. She looked at her oldest son and said, "Jess, go get your Pa and tell him to hurry."

As the tall lanky boy jumped up and started running

to the barn, Jean looked again at what her unbelieving eyes could not imagine.

There, clutched in her son's fist, was the biggest wad of money she had every seen. She looked past his hand into what indeed was an old cotton sack and saw it was crammed full of green currency. Jean made a small gasp and fell backwards, making a soft sloshing sound as her butt landed in the rain soaked grass.

"Pa, Pa," Jess yelled as he ran into the barn where his Dad had just finished milking the cow.

"Come on Pa. Luke just found something and Ma wants you to come see it. Hurry." Phil sat the milk bucket down near the barn door and they ran from the bars. As they rounded the house, they saw Jean Morris lying on the ground. She was staring at the sky as if she were day dreaming. She was thinking, "We are rich. I'm gonna buy me a new wood stove. I'm gonna buy the children new shoes and clothes and Phil can buy that new plow he's always wanted and---and". All kind of good things were running through her mind.

Phil and Jess bent over her and Phil patted her cheek. "Jean, Jean, Are you alright?" Phil asked her.

"Oh! Yes, I'm alright." She practically screamed. "Just look in the sack. Oh, Phillip, we are rich! We're rich!"

As Phil look into the sack, he was surprised at all the money.

"Where did it come from? Whose is it? Am I dreaming? This can't be true. I must be having a dream," he thought, as he looked at his children pulling all the green stuff out of the sack.

"No, boys, keep it in the sack and put what you took out, back into the sack. We'll count it later." Phil said. Phillip loaded the sack onto his shoulder and made his was to the kitchen. With the dim light from the kerosene lamp that was sitting on the middle of the table. He was thinking all this time what he was going to buy with the money. He placed it on the table and said, "We must find out who this belongs to. Who around here has this much money?" They all began to think who it could belong to.

Luke said, "Some of it belongs to me. I found it."

Maybe I oughta go to town and see the sheriff." Phil said.

I don't think that's a good idee." Jean said. "It might belong to the moffie."

"Just what do you suppose we ortta do with it?" Phil asked.

"I think we ortta put some in the bank and keep some of it." Jean replied.

"Ok" he said. "That's what we will do. But first, we need to count it." He emptied the sack out on the kitchen table and sat sown in a chair because he thought he was going to faint. There were hundreds of dollar bills, twenty and fifty dollar bills all wadded together.

So many bright and happy thoughts were running through is mind, he could hardly speak. Finally he caught his breath and managed to call the children in to help sort it out. He tossed the old wet sack in the corner of the kitchen and began to straighten the bills.

Luke, being nosy, picked up the sack and a white piece of paper fell to the floor. As he picked it up, he said to his dad, "Pa, here are some papers still in the sack and they have some writing on them."

"Let me see them, son." Phillip replied. As Luke handed the papers to his dad, he asked, "Pa, do you think this is money, too?" "No, son, let me read it."

Jean came over to where Phillip was reading and bent over his shoulder so she could see the words better. As she began to read, her face had a frown on it. The happy and excited look on her face was gone.

"What does it say, Pa?" Luke asked noting the frown on his dad's face.

"Yeah, Pa, read it to us." Jess said. He was so excited with all the commotion that was going on.

After Jean had finished reading, she sat across the table from Phil and buried her face in her hands. "What an awful disappointment. All our dreams of what we could buy are all gone. I'll never get my new stove now." She was thinking.

"This money belongs to Mr. and Mrs. James Morton.

They live over on the other side of the river. I will take it to them in the morning. I know they must be worried to death about all their money gone. You boys put all the money back in the sack." Phillip said. Pouting and disappointed, they crammed it all back into the sack.

"Can I have some, Pa?" Luke asked. "I was the one that found it."

"No, son, it's not ours. It would be wrong to keep any of it." Pa said.

No one in the Morris family could sleep that night they were all thinking of the money and what they could do with it, if it belonged to them.

Returning The Money

As the sun was peeking its head above the horizon the next morning, it was like a ball of fire in the east. Phillip was hoping it would be a nice day. He had to fix the roof on the house, chicken house. He had so much work to do. He worked all day with the money on his mind. He did have a goodnights sleep for he was so exhausted from the hard day at work. Next morning bright and early he hitched the mules to the wagon at the crack of dawn and waited to see if the weather was going to be good for him to go to the other side of the river. He kissed Jean and the children, then he stuffed the sack of money underneath the wagon seat so it would be out of sight, waved to his family and with the reigns, he popped the mules on their rumps and said,

"Gitty-up, gitty-up." Down the road they ran with the wagon rattling and the mules huffing and a-puffing.

As he neared the old gravel road, he slowed the team down. It was too dangerous to go at full speed. The sky in the west was a pearly blue with the sun on his back he was glad he was going west to avoid the bright rising sun.

As he approached the river bridge, the mules slowed and balked on him, afraid to cross the river. "Get up, you ornery critters," he yelled as he slapped the reins across their backs. No amount of urging would make the mules go forward. Instead, they stood their ground only raising and lowering their strong legs and fidgeting back and forth. "I don't have time for this", Phillip thought as his mind reminded him of all the work that had to be done on his damaged farm and house. He looked ahead at the long bridge that crossed over the wide river and saw what his mules had already seen. There, coming from the other side of the bridge, were two dark black horses pulling a black shiny hearse.

The two strong stallions were charging forward. Tall black feathery plumes attached to their head gear were swept back in the wind as the death wagon crossed the bridge.

Sitting high on the seat of the hearse, all dressed in black, was the town's one and only undertaker, old man Floyd. As he neared, Phillip could see him plainly. He was a tall man, well over six feet, but thin as a rail. His cheeks were hollowed and his dark eyes sank back into his head making him resemble a living, breathing skull. Atop his head was his ever-present all stove pipe hat.

As the undertaker pulled close to Phillip and his old wagon, he slowed the two large horses to a slow walk and finally stopped next to Phillip. He nodded slightly and said, "'Morning, Mr. Morris", and gave him a slight smile. As he did, his large teeth (whom many said came from a Sears and Roebuck catalogue) only emphasized the illusion of a skeleton all dressed in black.

"Good morning, Mr. Floyd", Phillip answered, "I

13

sure didn't expect to see anybody out this was so early in the morning."

"Oh, you can't sleep in my business, son. If you snooze, the buzzards get fat." He half way chuckled, "Been over to the Morton's. You know their house was took away by the twister yestiddy. Nothing but the chimney left. Their neighbor, young Kenny, found Morton and his misses in his corn field, dead to the world. Funny, they was holding hands, couldn't hardly pry'em apart." and this time he did grin and Phillip realized why all the town youngins crossed the street before they got to old man Floyd's parlor. He looked at the huge old hearse with its glass sides and black lacy curtains to hide its contents within, but he could still see the covered budges that were certainly James and Janice Morton. A shutter ran down his spine. These were the very people he was on his was to see.

"Well, I gotta be on my way now, young Morris." the tall man said, nodding toward the back of the hearse. "These two don't need any more heat than they already got." With that he gave a slight tap to the reins and the two huge black stallions charged forward with their morbid load of death.

Phillip sat there wondering, "What in the world should I do now?" He turned and watched the undertaker as he drove his team and wagon down the road. The glossy black hearse trimmed in shiny silver, glimmered in the morning sun.

Phillip turned his mule around and sat there watching the big black plumes on the stallions head and the hearse. The big black plumes lay back like a huge bird and the silver on the reigns and the hearse were ever so bright as the sun shone on them. He watched until they were clean out of sight. "Poor Morton and Janice, hey never can spend any of their fortune now, but I sure can." He thought. He then looked back over at the river and the bridge. The river running ever so swiftly and the old wooden bridge with its weather beaten planks were to be something of the past to him. He was going to live a good life from now on.

The sun beaming down on him was so hot, he

looked up and down the road and no one was in sight. Down the road he saw an old oak tree that must have been a hundred years old. He popped the mules with the reigns and they began to head for home. When he neared the old oak tree, he pulled back on the reigns and said, "Whoa, whoa," and they stopped suddenly causing the bag of money to roll from under the seat. He stepped down from the wagon and walked to the tree.

"Just what am I going to do with this?" Phillip thought to himself. He looked down at the ground, kicked rocks and clots of dirt, worried to death, not know just what to do. A bee was swarming around his face. He took off his hat and swatted at it. His balding head was wet with sweat as was his shirt. Looking at the trees, up in the sky and all the surrounding brush and rubble, he slowly crawled back onto the wagon and then he patted the bag of money and said, "All you big ones, you are mine now."

He had his mind made up and he knew what he would do, so he said, "Gitty-up, oh, gitty-up." The mules were on their way home now. He sat straight up and held his head high as if he were a millionaire. He was at that moment, a big millionaire.

He was looking at all the destruction and rubble from the storm as he passed each home place. The Burton home was completely gone; only the hen house was left. He saw little Jim's little red wagon in the pasture. He said to himself, "How lucky we are." Good things to buy were on his mind now. "One of these days I'ma gonna have me a big, big Tobacker farm."

When Phil was nearing home, he began to get nervous. As he turned the team into his place, he went straight to the barn. Hurriedly, pulling the bag out of the wagon he rushed to a stall in the barn, with his foot he raked some straw and manure from beneath a manger. With all the speed he could muster, he then pushed the bag of money under the manger and again with his foot he covered the bag with the same straw and manure that he had just raked out. He had to hurry because the family was all coming out to meet him. A pain, which he thought was indigestion, hit him hard in the chest. He hit himself hard in the chest with his fit, trying to make himself belch, but to no avail.

"Luke, will you take care of the mules? Please?" He asked his young son.

"Yes sir," Luke replied.

Walking back to the house, Jess, being the nosy one asked," Pa, did Mr. James" at that very moment Phillip turned to Jess and pointed his finger at him, he said," don't any of you ask any questions, that goes for you too, Ma. Do you hear me?"

"Yes, Sir," they said as they ran around the house to play ball. When Luke came into the house, he told him the same thing.

As they were walking to the house Jean said," Did you hear that? The funeral Bell is ringing, what is going on Phil? Who's it for?"

Phil looked into her troubled face," It's the Morton's he said, they died in the storm. I met the undertaker on my way over to their place."

" Oh, my Lord," she said, those poor people, they

were the kindest old folks I know." Then she thought of her husband's trip.

"Phil," she said," that's where you were headed, what did you do? What about the money?" Phil placed his fingers on his wife's lips," SSSHHH," he said, " I've have it hid, but I don't want to hear anything else about it. I'm thinking and besides me and Jess got to go into town and help dig the graves. Just don't worry about it, think about it or mention it again, do you hear me? Right now, Jess and I have to be on our way to town and help dig two graves.

Journey To The Graveyard

Meanwhile, the two black stallions were well on their way to the church and cemetery. They were hot and thirsty with foam running out their mouths. Both had so much slobber, one shook his head real hard and something hit old man Floyd's cheek. He thought a bird had flown over.

He pulled out his handkerchief and wiped his face. The white hankie was full of slobber from the horse.

As they turned into the church yard, a big vat of water was just inside the yard. He drove his team that was pulling the Death Wagon to the vat and said, "Here old boys I know you need this, so just help yourselves." He let the horses drink their fill and traveled on up to the Parsonage. It was a very small white house sitting next to the church.

No one had informed the pastor of the Polk Baptist Church and cemetery that a funeral and burial would be today. When the two black stallions pulled the hearse in to Pastor Martin's yard, he with his walking cane in one hand and the Holy Bible in the other hand opened the screen door and motioned to Bro. Floyd to come in. Pastor Martin was a big heavy set man with a week worth of beard and his hair was thick, black and beginning to turn grey, he had the meanest black eyes you would ever see. When he smiled his teeth were brown from the tobacco he was chewing and tobacco juice was running down his chin on each side of his mouth.

Old man Floyd told him he had two bodies that needed to be put in the ground.

"Two at one time?" he asked,

Then he put his parted fingers to his mouth and spat tobacco juice through them.

"Yes, they were killed in the storm day before yesterday." Mr. Floyd answered.

"Let me see what I can do," Pastor Martin said, as he was walking over to where a big black Bell was hanging. His feeble old hands were shaking like a leaf being blown by the wind, he put the Bible in the chair that was by the bell and hung his cane on the post of the chair. It took both hands to ring the bell.

Constant ringing of the Bell meant a fire, everyone comes to help----a slow ring meant a wedding, no need to come to town----of course there was ringing at Easter, at Christmas and on the fourth of July, but that was normal, and then there was the fifteen. Fifteen rings, three slow rings with a pause and then three more with a pause and three more until it rang fifteen times. That meant a death and every able bodied man was to come and help dig the graves of the burial.

The pastor grabbed the rope and started the signal everyone dreaded. The men in their fields plowing the ground and the ones that were cutting timber for new ground stopped what they were doing and went to the church to help. They knew that fifteen rings of the bell meant a grave needed to be dug.

The men and their sons all showed up to help. When Phillip and Jess got to the graveyard there was already a crowd there. They were dressed in their faded overalls with one strap unbuttoned and hanging down and their old red checked shirts and Brogan shoes on. All had brought their pickaxes and shovels, when each one arrived they went to the grave spot and began to dig. Within the hour the two graves were dug and the men gathered and decided the funeral would be at three o'clock that afternoon. They were afraid to wait till the next day for fear the bodies would be stinking and smelling bad from all the heat. With that taken care of they all went home.

The two Oak coffins that the undertaker had made were setting stately above the holes the town's men and farmers had dug earlier that morning.

The whole town was gathered for the services of James and Janice Morton.

All the men who had been grungy and dirty that

morning, were now in their Sunday best, shoes shined and hair slicked back. Brother Martin had actually shaved and was in full voice as he conducted the double funeral. He spoke of the Mortons; how kind and generous they were and how honest they were. He told of how Janice had sold him a dozen eggs one time, how she counted each one of them out of the basket but there was only eleven eggs and she deducted two cents off the price. No more honest and decent folks had he known.

Phil was listening to the preacher but only slightly. He was looking around at his neighbors and friends. There next to the Jones's was the banker, Don Rush, he was clearly the best dressed man there and Phil was wondering if he knew about the Morton's selling their farm, if he was expecting them to bring in a large sum of money for him to look after. He looked over at Sheriff Johnson standing there with his badge shining in the afternoon Sun and a large revolver strapped to his hip. Could he be expecting the Sheriff to question him, after all old man Floyd had seen him near the

Morton's farm. Could he be sent to prison for keeping the money that was not his? He glanced over at his family, Jean standing there in her old Paisley dress, faded but clean. "When's the last time Jean had a new dress," he wondered to himself. The three children were dressed in their best clothes but he noticed they were tattered with patches that Jean had carefully sewn over the holes.

Little Annie was standing next to her mother with her Raggedy Ann doll clutched in her arms. Phil saw tears streaming down her cheeks and he remembered that Janice Martin had been her Sunday School Teacher and had often brought the youngins homemade cookies.

Finally the preacher was concluding the services. He asked everyone to join him in the Lord's Prayer and the town folk slowly walked away from the two coffins. Phil stayed behind. He and several other men were to lower the coffins and cover the graves. One by one they lowered the coffins to their final resting place.

Later that evening the Morris family sat around the

dinner table everyone was quiet and only a few words were spoken. Phil's mind now was on this meager supper of ham, beans and cornbread and he was thinking that soon they would be eating like kings.

When bedtime came Phil lay next to his wife but things were still strangely silent. His mind was once again keeping him awake.

"What should I do?" He wondered.

If we start spending money now folks will wonder. Someone may become suspicious. Whoever bought the Morton farm may wonder what happened to the money.

"Could I go to prison for this?" His mind went over and over the possibilities until he finally decided on one thing. He would hid the money and not touch it for a year. By then ever thing would be forgotten and he could use it and get the things he and his family dreamed of-----and he knew the perfect place for him to hide it!!

Kept Secret

Phillip tossed and turned all night, sleep was not on his mind the ordeal that lay ahead of him was on his worried mind.

Making sure Jean was sound asleep, he eased himself out of bed carefully picking up his old dirty brogan shoes and his overalls, he tip toed out to the back porch and dressed.

Carefully he slipped to the barn. He put the saddle on old Mollie, his mule and hurriedly uncovered the sack that was under the manger. Shaking the dirt and manure off the sack, he put it on Mollies back, grabbed the old rusty shovel, and then pulled himself into the saddle. Being quite as he possibly could he urge Mollie from the barn being ever so careful not to wake Jake, the dog? Very slowly he and Mollie made it to the cotton field. They kept close to the fence that separated the cotton field from the forest, speeding up the pace a little, he heard the owls and all the critters in the woods next to him, and he suddenly got an awful sharp pain in his chest. "Oh, I got that gas again, I'll take some of Jeans baking soda and water when I get back to the house" he thought to himself. He had been having these sharp pains for a few weeks.

Far behind the cotton field stood an old oak tree, over a hundred years old. He knew where he would to put the money. As he neared the tree, he slowed Mollie to a stop. He lowered himself to the ground, looking at the huge boulder that had been under the tree for years and years.

That was where he would hide the money, underneath that big rock. He pushed and pulled on the rock but could not budge it. He decided to sit on the big rock and rest for a while. Looking up toward the cloudless blue heavens with dimly lit stars he said, "Lord, forgive me for what I'm about to do. You know

I'm doing this for my wife and kids. So they will have a better life next year."

After a few minutes of rest he said to himself.

"I'll just get the shovel and bury it here between the rock and the tree; no one will ever know it's a way out here "he said, talking to himself. Phil was forever talking to himself when he was alone. Rushing as fast as he could, he buried his treasure and climbed upon Mollie and headed for the house. He was exhausted and hungry, thinking of all the things he would buy next year. The sun would soon be up, it was getting light over in the east, and he prodded Mollie to go faster. When they finally reached the barn, he unsaddled Mollie as fast as he could. He didn't want Jean to know what he had been doing. He turned Mollie lose and started walking slowly toward the house. "This blame indigestion is about to kill me ", he thought to himself. "What's wrong with me"? His mind wandered to his dad and how he had died at an early age. Bad heart the doctors had said, "But I'm strong", he thought, "My hearts alright. I farm. I work the fields. I'm as healthy as a horse. It's gotta be all this stress. I've been through a tornado, dug two graves, dug a hole for my money and all the worries that it's caused. I'm just worn out, need some rest". He suddenly stumbled and fell to the ground.

Jean Morris always arose early. Some times before Phil, sometimes not. This morning she noticed Phil had gotten up before her. Sliding the bedroom curtains apart, she marveled at the beautiful morning before her. The sun was just rising and the trees were full of singing birds. From the back yard she heard the roosters crowing and giggling to herself thinking, "Your late old boys." Humming to herself, Amazing Grace, she went to the kitchen and started her morning routine.

"I hope Phil brings in some fresh eggs," she thought, and put the coffee pot on the stove to boil. When the coffee was done, Jean slid the big iron skillet to the edge of the stove to reduce the heat. The sizzling bacon was almost done and she wanted some fresh eggs to fry. She briefly checked the biscuits and then went to the back door to call her husband. She opened the door and looked toward the barn, just as she was about to yell for Phil she saw him lying on the ground. Jean ran across the back yard screaming Phil's name. As she got to his feeble body she gently took his shoulders in her hands and turned him over. Kneeling she placed his head in her lap and stroked his hair. "Phil," she cried, "what's wrong, what's wrong"?

Jess appeared at the back door still in his longjohns he hollered, "Ma, what's going on? Is Pa alright? Jean looked at her son and screamed, "Hurry, Jess, get dressed, get Mollie and go fetch Doc Baker. There is something bad wrong with your Pa, I think he is about gone. "Hurry, son, hurry."

Jess hurriedly dressed, raced across the yard, jumped on old Mollie, goosed her and headed for town.

Jean looked down at her husband, his eyes were closed and his forehead was wrinkled with pain. Sadly she gently stroked his cheeks and said, "Phil, Phil, wake up! Don't you die on me, Phil Morris." In her mind she knew he had died. "What's next? How will we ever get along and make it without Phil? Where is all that money, and what did he do with it? Guess we will never know. I will never get my new stove, now." She kissed her husband's head and began to sob. "What will we do now? How will I tell the children? Where is the money" she was thinking.

No one will ever know where the money is. What a mystery. It will be a long, long time before it will ever be found, IF EVER.

Never Again

As the hot summer sun was sinking low in the west just above the horizon it was like a big red ball of fire. Jess, was sitting alone in a swing in the backyard, as Alice his wife was in the kitchen preparing his supper.

Jess's mind drifted back to the times when he was a young boy. He was thinking of his mom, dad, brother, sister and the old homestead he grew up on. In

Jess and Alice had a very nice comfortable home in the outskirts of Indianapolis. Their lives were almost perfect. They had two wonderful boys named Johnny and Donald.

The siren of the fire engine, police, the railroad trains whistle blowing and the busy streets, was something they were accustomed to now.

His mind kept going back to the quite peaceful house on the farm. He remembered the smell of the cotton fields with dew on them early each morning. Oh, how he longed to go back and see the old home place. It had been many years since he had been there.

Jess was selected to go to war. Only three months into basic training his mother passed away. His father had passed away when Jess was only a small child. He hasn't seen the old homestead since that time. Shortly after his parents both died his first son, Johnny was born. He and Alice were very happy parents. As he sat there in the swing, his eyes were focused on some ants on the ground, traveling back and forth to a small mound they had built on the ground. Jess, was day dreaming about the good old days when he was a young boy.

" Supper is ready, Jess" Alice said as she stepped outside the screen door she had just painted that morning." The paint is still wet" she said.

"I'm coming, I was just thinking" he said.

"Thinking about what?" Alice asked,

"The old home place, down south."

As they entered the kitchen the aroma of roasted beef filled the air "What a wonderful cook she is. She cooks just like my mother except she doesn't hum." he was thinking.

As he sat at the table he was still thinking of the old home place. His brain was blogged with the good old times, when he was a young lad.

After they had finished dinner, and Alice was clearing the table, Jess, was talking to Johnny and Donald and telling them about the good old times he had, when he was a boy, out on the farm in Mississippi. They were so excited, to listen to their dad's tales, even though they had heard them so many times before. It was still amazing to them and they wanted to see the place their dad had grown up on. Johnny asked his dad, " Dad, do you still own that farm?"

"Yes, son, we still own it, why do you ask? Johnny said," When school is out, can all of us go to the farm? Can we dad?" At that very moment Donald chimed in," Yeah, dad, can we? I bet that would be fun. Please, dad." Jess was so thrilled the boys wanted to go the farm. That night as Jess and Alice lay in bed, they talked about going to the farm when school was dismissed for the summer. Next morning, they told the boys the family was going to the farm for two weeks, soon as school was out. The boys were filled with excitement because school would be out the next Friday.

Vacation

Alice had packed the travel trailer with all sorts of camping equipment. Everything they would need for a week or two. The boys brought their fishing gear and slingshots. They were amazed at the scenery along the highway, it was a long and tiresome trip but no one complained. They were so happy all kind of good visions were going through their minds.

When they neared the vicinity that Jess knew as a child, the entire countryside was so unfamiliar, nothing seemed the same. The dirt and gravel roads were all paved and were two lanes. The old wooden bridge over the river was gone and a new bridge had been built which was four-lane. Beautiful homes have been built on the highway near the farm.

Jess, could hardly believe his eyes when he found the home place. Beautiful homes have been built on the highway near the farm. As they rounded the curve and saw the old house Jess, eyes filled with tears. They were tears of joy.

After Luke and Annie died, the place was left to Jess. He hired a real estate agent to take care of the house and do what was necessary. The house now had city water and electricity and a bathroom had been added. The old outhouse was gone but the barn was still in good shape. Jess saw some hollyhocks his mother had planted years ago. They were at each side of the back door. A single red rose bush was still in the front yard. Jess, just stood there looking around without saying a word. He was just thinking, how things were when he was a kid.

After looking inside the house they decided to spend their vacation there. It was very late in the afternoon and they had to unload the trailer that held all their groceries, cots, clothing and fishing gear. Next morning they all went out exploring the farm. What used to be the cotton field was now grown trees. How strange things looked to Jess. Pointing his finger to the East and speaking to the boys he said," There is a pond over there somewhere." Maybe we can go fishing, dad," Donald said. Jess, was wondering where the neighbors were. Had they all moved or passed away? There were so many things running through his mind and questions to be answered.

The next morning as the family sat on the front porch they were planning what to do. The sky was overcast with clouds and it looked as though it would start to rain any minute. Far away in the woods a dove was calling its mate. The sound of a dove cooing seemed so sad." Jess listened to that," doesn't it sound lonesome?" Jess remarked.

The boys were anxious to get to the woods but were afraid they would get lost if they were by themselves. After about three days the boys knew every path and trail in the woods and on the farm. They decided to go exploring alone and leave mom and dad by themselves for a while, after all they were two teenagers and knew were they could and could not go. They just wanted to be alone for a while and do what boys do best, explore.

As they walked through the barn and looked at all the stalls and mangers, they even climbed to the loft.

After leaving the barn, Johnny being the oldest picked up a long stick and used it as a staff. Donald had to follow suit and found one too. They just strolled along looking at the trees and leaves and birds and anything that moved. As they got deep into the woods it was very quiet except for the insects, birds and squirrels making their own noises.

Donald began to get tired and wanted to rest. "I'm going to rest here by this old tree, you go on and look around but come back here to get me and we will go to the house" Donald told Johnny.

"Okay, I won't be gone long" Johnny said.

One side of the old tree was covered with green moss as was a big boulder that was half buried beneath the tree. Donald sat down and leaned backward on the tree. Looking up in the tree, to his surprise was a family of squirrels, playing and running on every limb of the tree. Donald remained very still, and quite, just watching the squirrels as one little bushy tailed squirrel raced down the tree. When the little squirrel got within about 3 feet from Donald, it came to a sudden stop, was switching its tail and watching Donald. A few minutes passed and like a bullet he turned around and high tailed it back up the tree. Donald was so amazed at the squirrels he wouldn't move just watched. The little squirrel scurried up the tree trunk and out on the limb as if to hide himself. He was lying flat on a rather large limb. Waiting for a little while, the squirrel peeked over the limb and looked at Donald. Within the blink of an eye, he would jerk his head back and peek over the other side of the limb. He did this for several minutes and finally stopped checking on Donald.

An adult squirrel came down the backside of the tree and made its way to the big boulder. Just looking around he found an old acorn, sat on his back legs and with his front feet held the nut and nibbled at it. When the little squirrel had eaten his food he began to dig around in the ground. He found an old piece of cloth and was pulling on it. Donald, thought," What in the world has that squirrel found?" Fast as lightning the squirrel ran up the tree. Donald being curious about it went over to the boulder. There was part of an old rag that looked as though more than one squirrel had been pulling on it. When Johnny returned, Donald, told him about the squirrel that played peep-eye with him, the one that ate the acorn and about the rag the squirrel tried to pull out of the ground. As boys do, curiosity got the best of them and they went over to the rag. With all their might they tried to pull the old cloth but with no success. They gave up and went home. Keeping it a secret, the next morning they got a shovel and went to the same spot and began to dig up the old rotten cloth. What did they expect to find? What might be in that ground? Why did they want to dig it up? Just being boys. While digging, they found earthworms. They thought about going fishing with them, but had no way to take them home.

"Maybe, we can go fishing tomorrow." Donald said.

Yeah, let's get up early in the morning and go to the pond." Johnny replied. Handing Donald the shovel Johnny said," Here, you dig, while I check out the squirrels. Johnny was always the one to shun work. He would get Donald to do all the dirty work, and wait on him as if he was younger than Donald. Donald always fell for his smooth talking.

Donald got the best of him one day.

This is what happened

Each afternoon as they arrived home from school, Johnny would be the first one to turn on the TV and watch what he wanted. Donald would make a sandwich and take it to the TV room. Johnny always asked him for half of his sandwich, which Donald would half it and hand it to Johnny. One day Donald made a special sandwich. He made a sandwich out of dog food put it on the plate and took it to Johnny. Without taking his eyes off the TV he picked up his sandwich and ate it. Donald was watching him as he took his last bite.

"Did you like that sandwich, Johnny?" Donald asked him.

"Yes, Donald. It was very good, thank you". Johnny replied. Laughingly, Donald started for the door saying," that was Kam dog food you ate, Johnny" Johnny never said a word and never took his eyes off the TV set. He acted as if he didn't hear a word that Donald had been saying. From that day on he never asked Donald the fix him a sandwich or if he could have half of his. Donald was so thrilled that he had pulled that over on Johnny.

Donalds Discovery

Donald was busy digging up the old rag that turned out to be an old cotton sack. Exhausted, he pulled the old sack out of the ground and all its contents. He opened the old bag and could not believe his eyes.

"Am I dreaming, is this real," he was thinking to himself. He looked around for Johnny which had his head up in the air looking at the squirrels." Johnny, Johnny, come quick and look at what I found." Donald yelled. Johnny started walking slowly to where Donald was. His eyes still on a squirrel that was sitting on a limb, high the old oak tree, "Come on," Donald yelled in an aggravated voice. Johnny was one that never got in a hurry. He was always the last one to get on the school bus.

Donald was beginning to get upset. When Johnny's eyes got a glimpse all the green stuff that Donald was holding he began to get nervous.

"This is a lot of money" Johnny said." What are we going to do with it? Let's just split it and not tell anyone about it. We would be rich. We would be two rich Morris boys."

Donald was so upset with Johnny. He could not understand what had come over Johnny. "No, we need to take this to mom and dad" Donald said in a very sarcastic manner. Johnny was so disappointed but went along with Donald. They wasted no time, they walked as fast as they could and took turns carrying the money. When they got to the house mom and dad were sitting on the porch. Racing up the steps, being so excited, Donald dropped the old dirty bag in his mother's lap.

"Just look here what we have found" Johnny said as he was trying the opened the bag. Jess, rising from his chair and his eyes were wide open as if they were going to pop out of his head.

"Where did you find this?" The dad asked. The boys told the story of the squirrels and the old Oak tree and the boulder that was underneath it, and about the squirrel pulling on the old rag. Jess knew exactly where the tree was with the boulder beneath it.

They poured the money on the table and began to count it. Suddenly, Jess saw a white piece of paper that had begun to turn yellow. When he read what was on the paper his eyes filled with tears, he looked at Alice and each of the boys. They could tell by the expression on his face that something bad was wrong.

"What is it, honey?" Alice asked. She rushed to get a wet cloth to wipe his brow." Are you all right now?"

"Yes, I'll be all right now but I have a lot to tell all of you" Jess answered.

He began telling the story about the mighty storm that came through Polk County when he was just a young boy. He remembered how he and Luke had found the money many years ago. How his dad had stowed it away and never told anyone where it was. It was such an electrifying story all the family had tears beginning to weld up in their eyes.

Jess just sat there mortified, thinking of all the things that happened at that farm so many years ago.

"What are we going to do with this Jess?" Alice asked.

"Let me think for a while and we will come up with something." Jess replied.

His mind was filled with so many memories and then this money was another problem for him to worry about.

Jess, didn't sleep a wink that night he had such mixed emotions his childhood went over and over in his mind. It was just so sad. He tossed and turned all night. Thinking of the money his dad had put away, and how his mother wanted a new stove. He was happy to see the old place again but it caused him so much sadness he never wanted to see the place again.

The next morning while sitting at the breakfast table, everyone was calm and quite. Each one was waiting on another to speak. Not knowing what to say, each one held their peace.

It was dark and cloudy that day and they could hear thunder roaring in the West. It brought back memories of the mighty storm to Jess.

Finally, Jess spoke up saying," Well, I think I know what we should do now." Speaking to his two sons he said," your mom and I have decided to go into town and talk to the realtor about selling this place. I've enjoyed being here and seeing the old homestead once more, but it's so sad for me because I think of the times when I was a young boy and lived right here. Now, you boys have seen the farm that I grew up on."

Going Back Home

As Alice was hustling around getting things ready to pack to go home, they had only been there for a week and still had an extra week of their vacation. Jess's life was in such an unsettled condition, they thought it would be best to pack up and go home. The boys were disappointed but they went about their business helping to get things ready to go home.

Johnny asked Donald," where is the bag of money and how much is in it?"

Donald answered," I don't know dad did something with it."

When Jess came in the house it had begun to rain. He told his family, he thought it be best if they waited till morning to leave for home. The boys were happy about that and wanted to go to the woods in the rain. They were not allowed to go off in the woods but they could go play in the barn. They spent most of the day playing in the barn. When they got back to the house Alice was making dinner and told the boys to get their selves cleaned up. They did as they were told. When the family sat down to have dinner, Jess and Alice began to talk about the money. That was just what Johnny wanted them to do, he wanted to know where it was and, was he going to get any of it.

Johnny wanted to buy a four wheeler with some of the money. His friends that lived on Cornell Street had a four wheeler and he wanted one too.

Jess said," We have decided to put this money in the bank at home and keep it till you graduate from high school Johnny, then we will go and buy you a car. And Donald, when we get this place sold we will buy you a car with that money".

Both boys were happy about that but it would be a year before Johnny graduated. And it would be two years before Donald graduated, but they could wait that long. Johnny's thoughts were on a new four wheeler

The next morning they finished packing the trailer and looked the place over to make sure they were not leaving anything behind. They secured all the Windows and doors.

As they were pulling out of the drive onto the highway, all of them looked back at the old home place. It had been fun for the boys but for dad it had been misery. He looked in the rear view mirror to see the old home place for the last time, he was thinking," I never want to see this place again, never ever. "

They drove to town and found the realtor, asked him to put their place up for sale. They got their business finished with the real estate agent and started on the long trip back to Indianapolis.

Johnny asked," how much money do we have dad?"

"It's only $40,000. That was a lot back in the early 30s. All of it will be spent on you boys. They rode in silence most of the way home, speaking only when necessary.

Jess thinking, "Never again, never again, I never want to see this place ever again.

The Scarlet Angel

IT WAS IN the early 60s, before we had cell Phones and all the necessities we have today. TVs were just coming in full force. Not everyone owned a TV, but everyone wanted one. Even Lena Gray wanted one.

Lena Gray was somewhat of a loner. She lived on Oak Street, in a small apartment she had rented about three years ago.

When she arrived in town, she applied for a job at the local dry cleaners and was accepted as a clerk. She enjoyed her work and it paid well. She worked short hours at the cleaners.

After being in Jackson for quite a while, she started going to church and later joined the First Baptist Church of Jackson. She hardly ever missed a meeting, she sang in the choir, and was there every Sunday morning and Sunday evening and Wednesday evening for services she never missed a meeting or service unless she called the Pastor to let him know she wouldn't be there.

No one knew where she came from or if she had a family. She was just a beautiful blonde with a body that everyone noticed. She never dated and had been single all her life. The ladies of the church envied her because she was so beautiful, trim and proper. But they all were very nice to her. The men would sometimes make catty remarks about her to each other but that was alright with the men of the church.

All the people in Jackson wondered where she came from and who she really was. That caused them to have doubts. But all went well at the cleaners and at church. She was always dressed in the finest.

She stood tall with her blonde hair shining like gold as she stood in the choir singing. She was sure an asset to the church, what evil thoughts ran through her mind as the pastor was preaching or praying. As she sat in the choir loft she would scan each and every man in the congregation. She wondered how he would be if they were together. There was no man in that church she thought would be a good client.

No one knew what Lena did at night.

She worked at the dry cleaners from 9 am until 4 pm. Each day as she left work, she would go to her car and drive 25 miles to the next town that had a huge truck stop with a nice little café. She would park her car in the far north side of the parking lot, where the employees parked, to keep from being noticed. She would always eat dinner at the same table and wait for truckers who were lonely and tired, to come in and ask her out.

Each evening she would change clothes in her car, put on tight jeans and high heels and plenty of make-up. She then would comb her hair and just let it fly away. She would smile at all the men as they came in the café to eat. Everyone admired her and it didn't take long until a lonesome traveler would ask her if they could sit down with her. "Of course you may join me," she would say. After a short conversation a trucker would ask if she would like to see his truck .Of course she knew exactly what he meant. It didn't take long and afterward she would reenter the café. She would stroll to the same table as she had before and wait on another man to come in and ask her out. She would visit with three or four men each night until around 9:30pm or 10:00 pm. She would then drive back the 25 miles to her apartment. Upon arrival she would take a shower, count her money, and go to bed. She did this every night, except Sunday and Wednesday. Lena made money at the truck stop. She had regular customers. She didn't regard herself as a prostitute she was a lady of the night at the truck stop. She was a saint on Sunday and Wednesday. No one knew of her short comings and goings.

One Monday night in mid- April, she went to the

truck stop as usual, while sitting at her regular table a tall dark stranger walked in. "He sure is a handsome fellow." she thought to herself. She noticed his black hair, well groomed mustache and what beautiful blue eyes he had. He also had a gold chain with a cross on it around his neck. His pointy toed cowboy boots were so shiny; you could almost see yourself in them. He strolled over to the counter, taking long strides and ordered a cup of coffee. Lena thought to herself, what a handsome guy. As he turned around to look for a table he noticed Lena, sitting alone. He walked over to her table and introduced himself. He asked her, if she was all alone. She motioned for him to have a seat. He sat across the table from her and they began to talk about the weather, his truck and most everything in general, but most of all he talked about his truck and his job. As they were talking, he thought, "Hey, this is a high class hooker".

The handsome young fellow had just bought a brand new Peterbilt truck with a sleeper and all the necessities that a big semi- truck could have. After they were well acquainted, the handsome trucker invited Lena out to see his truck. As she stepped up in it, she gasped at the magnificent interior. It had all the nice things that made it look and feel so homey. She thought to herself, "This would be nice to take a trip in."

He slid under the wheel, as she was dressing in the sleeper. He asked her if she would like to go for a ride to the next little town. She was so excited to get to ride in the big truck.

When he revved up the engine, he also hit the knob and locked the doors. When they passed through the first little town, she began to get jittery. He reached into his pocket and held a little white pill in his hand, "Take this" he said. "It will make you feel better, it's only an aspirin." She did as he said, she took the aspirin with a sip of water rand swallowed it. In a very short while she was getting sleepy. He told her to go to the bed and get some rest he would take her back to the truck stop soon. She did as he told her and was soon fast asleep. He kept driving, but not to the truck stop. He was going across country and had gotten off his schedule so he had to make up time. Every time she would stir or make a noise, he would pull over to the side of the highway just long enough to give her another aspirin.

They went through many states that night and only stopped for fuel, fearing she might wake up. She had been asleep all night except when she woke and he would give her another aspirin. He kept pushing his new Peterbilt as fast as they possibly could go.

"It will soon be daybreak," he thought as he drove his big beautiful rig across the Mississippi River Bridge. The fog was so dense he had to pull over and stop. It was too dangerous to drive any further. Now stopped, he thought to himself, "I might as well take a nap with her." As he pulled back the blanket to ease into bed, her body was cold .He shook her to wake her but to no avail. She was dead, dead as a door nail. He started shaking and wondering, what in the world he was going to do. He knew immediately what had caused her death. It was the little white pills he had given her. He knew what he was going to do, he finally, made sure there was no traffic and the fog so thick, he unlocked the door on the passenger side and pushed her body to the ground. He was so afraid. He moved on even though the fog was like a mist. Just barely inching on, he didn't meet any traffic. When he made it through the next little town the fog had lifted and he went at full speed trying to make up for the time he had lost.

Back where he had dumped her body, the sun was coming up. A motorist came upon her and after getting out of his car, found she was dead. He went as fast as possible to get the police in the next little town. The police come and found she was dead and called the funeral home for the coroner to come. When the coroner got there, he pronounced her dead and called the funeral home for someone to come get the body. When they got the body to the funeral home, they searched her clothing for some kind of identification. She had no purse, no jewelry, no rings and the labels in her clothing had been removed.

No one knew her. So, who was she and where did she come from? Everyone wanted to know. She was ever so far from home. The police, radio stations and all that could, put out the news of the unknown. People from the city and surrounding towns came to the funeral home to view the body trying to identify her. No one had ever seen her before. The police had no leads on where she may have come from or who she might be. All anyone could say was, she sure was a beautiful lady, and then leave the funeral polar with a sad face.

Her death was all the people talked about around town and surrounding towns.

Lena Gray laid in the funeral home three weeks and her body needed to be buried. The undertaker called a pastor of a local church and asked if he would conduct a funeral for the unknown lady. The pastor was happy to help out with the funeral.

Lena Gray was laid to rest in a pauper's grave in the Union County Cemetery. The cemetery put a small headstone on her grave that read, "R.I.P. UNKNOWN, JANE DOE."

No one ever knew who she was or where she came from. The people of the church she attended missed her at each service. The men at the truck stop missed the beautiful lady of the night. Lena Gray lived a secret life, an angel in the daylight and a harlot at night.

May Lena Gray rest in peace!

Murder At Midnight

JACOB NEWSOM WAS a very inspiring and upcoming young dentist. He was making a big name for himself and his family. He was a very handsome and energetic young gentleman. He had been married to Linda for six years. Linda was a registered nurse that worked at the Memorial Hospital. She and Jay had two beautiful children ages five and two.

Jay and Linda were sweethearts in high school and went on to college together. Soon after they graduated from college they married, bought a beautiful home in gated community by the lake. It was a dream home to them.

It didn't take very long for Jay to have his dental practice up and going, with a big shingle over his front door that read JACOB NEWSON D.D.S. He was the only dentist in the town. His office was full of patients most of the time. Jay was a proud man, proud of his business, his wife and children.

The Newsom's were very impressive and soon became acquainted with the elite of the city. They join the country club and Jay was on the golf course every chance he got. The town folks knew Jay and believed him to be a very good asset to the small town they lived in. He was a very handsome man with jet black hair and a black mustache that made his big blue eyes sparkle. When he smiled his teeth were perfect, pearly white. All the ladies always took a second look at him. Linda was a small petite lady, with fair complexion and long flowing blonde hair, a beautiful lady in her late 20s.

Linda went back to work at the Memorial Hospital

after their two year old son was born. The only free time she and Jay had together was at night after they both got home from work or after meetings they had to attend. As time went on and the business grew, Jay hired a dental hygienist to help him. Her name was Jane McCroy. Jane was a very beautiful young lady and Jay seemed to have an eye for her.

Jane had been working at the dental clinic for about two months when Jay invited her out for dinner. She thought Dr. Jay was so handsome she accepted the invitation. After that dinner Jay seemed to have quit a few more meetings to attend than usual, more than Linda. Some of Jay's meetings lasted until early in the morning hours. Linda would always be asleep when he got home. He would always wake her and tell her all about the meetings about who was there and who said what and when. Linda loved Jay and put all her faith and love and belief and trusted in everything he would tell her. His meetings began to get more frequent and Linda began to get suspicious. They were a very happy couple with everything a young couple could ever wish for, but Linda was uneasy. She never said a word to Jay about all his meetings. Her heart was breaking because she knew something was wrong, he was having just too many meetings and they lasted longer than she thought they should.

In the spring of 2004 their perfect life changed.

The children were across town spending the night and day with Linda's parents. The grandparents were always glad when the children came to spend time with them, as all grandparents do.

That evening Linda arrived home before Jay and began making dinner for him. She had big plans for him that night. She had sat the table with the best China they had, had a fresh bouquet of flowers on the table with candles and wine glasses. It was going to be a wonderful night for her and Jay. She stood back away from the table and admired the setting. Linda thought to herself, "This will be a perfect night. It will be so romantic to be alone with Jay. It is going to be special".

After she had the table just the way she wanted

it, she finished preparing the meal of roast beef with potatoes and carrots, which was Jay's favorite. When she had everything in order and was pleased with the setting, she went upstairs and showered, and put the most intoxicating perfume on her naked body. She went to the closet and picked the sexy dress she had just bought, slipped it on and put her makeup on to perfection and let her hair down. She wanted to be exciting and beautiful for Jay when he got home. She was so delighted she would be alone with Jay .She admired herself in the mirror thinking," he will think I'm beautiful and sexy then take me in his arms and kiss me." All happy things were running through her mind. When she had everything perfect she went downstairs to wait for her lover.

Jay was late getting home that night. It was almost midnight when he arrived home and Linda was so disappointed and hurt, because he didn't call her or let her know that he would be so late. He thought she would be in bed asleep as usual. When he entered the house and saw Linda, how beautiful she was. He looked around at the table with candles and China on it and smelled the aroma of roast beef immediately he got upset. He yelled at her saying" what the hell do you think you're doing? Are you expecting your boyfriend over or has he already been here? Linda could tell by the look on his face that he was very, very mad. She could smell liquor on his breath and she began to get nervous and scared." No, no." she said as she began to cry. How disappointed she was. Jay slapped her and she began to yell, as she did he started beating her with his fist. Linda was struggling to get away but it made him more furious. He had knocked her to the floor and straddled her body and began to choke her until she had no breath. He suddenly realized what he had done, he had choked her to death, killed her. But that was what he wanted, wasn't it? He wanted her out of his way so he had killed the girl that loved him so very much; the mother of his children.

The ordeal frightened him so much he was out of breath and lazily sat in a chair and gazed at her limp body lying on the floor. He was thinking, "What in the world am I going to do now? What must I do? What can I do? At least I'm rid of her now. " He could feel the blood rush to his head and he began to feel dizzy.

As time passed he picked her limp body up from the floor and struggled up the staircase with her. He took her to the bathroom and put her body in the bath tub. He undressed her, then went downstairs to the kitchen and found a big butcher knife, lit a cigarette and went back upstairs. When he stepped inside the bathroom her body looked as though she was just asleep, how beautiful she was. He put his cigarette out in the ashtray that was on the dressing table. Slowly he turned and kneelt down by the bath tub.

His heart was beating fast and hard as he began his dirty job of dismembering her body. First her head then her arms and legs. When he had finished butchering her body he washed all the blood down the drain and washed her as if she was an animal. He rose from the bath tub he had been kneeling at, looked down at her body and said to her" now I can have my Jane all to myself no one will ever know where you will be. Jane and I will finally be happy." Jane was his dental hygienist. She had worked for him almost a year. He had fallen in love with Jane. He went back to the kitchen and got some big black plastic garbage bags. He picked her dismembered body up one piece at a time and put it in the bag. He then took the bags downstairs to the kitchen and made room in the chest type freezer for all the bags. Jay emptied the food from the freezer and put Linda in the bottom of it and covered her with the frozen food. If anyone looked in the freezer they would never know Linda's body was in the bottom of the freezer. Then he went upstairs and cleaned the bathroom till it looked like nothing had happened. He was satisfied with the way it looked.

Slowly he made his way downstairs to the table that Linda had so happily prepared for him. He sat at the table and ate his dinner and drank a big bottle of wine. He was doing some deep thinking. "Guess I better check to see if the freezer is locked." He didn't want anyone to look in the freezer. He locked it and then went upstairs and went to bed as usual as if he had not done one thing wrong.

Next morning he showered and went to work as usual but Linda didn't report in for work at the hospital. The receptionist at the hospital called the Newsom home but got no answer. Then she called Jay at work and told him Linda didn't come to work." Is anything wrong?"

Jay told the hospital receptionist that Linda had left by herself last night and never came back. Jay called Linda's parents before he went to work and asked if they could keep the children. He told them what happened. They came over to the home to look for Linda. Mrs. Oakman, Linda's mother, noticed Linda's car was still in the garage. Her personal belongings were still there. Her purse, jewelry and clothing were in their usual place.

Mrs. Oakman turned to her husband Louis and said" just what do you think of this Louis? What do you make of all this? She began to get worried for Linda safety.

." I'm not sure yet, but something fishy is going on here. Linda would never leave her children and just walk off."

"What must we do now, Louis? She asked.

"I think we need to call the police in on this" he answered. Jay didn't seem to be very concerned about her disappearance. The news went swiftly through town. It made the town folks disturbed that she could just vanish.

Mrs. Oakman immediately called the police. The law enforcement came out and searched the place and talk to Mr. in Mrs. Oakman. They went upstairs and looked in every nook and cranny they could find, but nothing was out of order. They went back down stairs and took their time searching ever where. They looked in the freezer and saw nothing but food. The police went to Jay's dental office and spoke with him.

He told them what he had been telling everyone else, that she just walked off. They noticed Jay was not very concerned and wondered why he was so calm.

The whole town was very disturbed that she could just disappear without a trace.

Mrs. Oakman knew Jay and Linda's neighbor that lived next door. Mary and her husband Bob were close friends of Jay and Linda's .

There was a tall wooden privacy fence with a gate in the middle that was built between Mary and Linda's homes. Mary and Linda always used the back doors to go visit each other. Mary and Linda are very good pals and went shopping together and told each other secrets as good friends do.

Mrs. Oakman went to visit Mary and tell her the news of Linda. Mary was very upset to learn her best friend was missing.

It was a dark and gloomy day with the wind blowing and a few drops of rain here and there. It didn't keep the two ladies from hurrying across the back lawn to Linda's house. As they entered the house Mary had a strange feeling to come over her. A feeling as though Linda was still there. It frightened Mary, she could feel Linda's presents nearby as they went from room to room, trying to find any evidence that would lead them to Linda or where she might be. Mary searched the bathroom. There was nothing out of order, she did notice Linda's new dress she had recently bought was lying in a heap on the floor and Mary began to wonder why. Linda would never leave her new dress lying on the floor. Mary began to get nervous and sick to her stomach and told Mrs Oakman she needed to go home. As she opened the back door she could feel Linda near her .What a strange feeling it was. "Where is she, I know she is some place near me, I feel her" Mary thought. A cold shiver came over Mary as she walked across the lawn to her house .She was filled with wonder and awe as she realized that Linda was in bad trouble and was nearby. Not knowing just what, but felt that Jay had something to do with this mystery.

Mary told Bob about Linda and her strange feelings. How she could feel her and she felt Linda was so close. Bob had an uneasy feeling as he sat listening to Mary. "Mary, I think it would be wise for you to tell the authorities about this.

Pondering on the elusions in her mind, Mary with shaky hands picked up the phone and called the police.

As the sheriffs car stopped in front of their house, two brawny uniformed policemen, one was the sheriff, came knocking on her door .They were sure impressive with their shiny badges and perfectly pressed blue uniforms on. They were pleasant looking gentlemen, one kept his hand on his hip covering his pistol. As Bob invited them in they removed their hats.

Mary explained to each of the policemen what she felt and her thoughts. They knew of Linda's disappearance, the department had already talked to Jay. They advised Mary to talk to Jay, let them know if anything came up that she thought was important to the case. They discussed where Linda might be and what might have happened to her.

The Sheriff said, "We can't go over there and search the place without a warrant as of this time" as they rose to leave. "We will stay on top of this matter and we thank you for your cooperation" they hurried to their cruiser and slowly pulled away.

About three days after Linda's disappearance Mary decided to pay Jay a visit trying to comfort him. Jay had built a big patio around the huge old oak tree that was in his backyard. That is where Jay and Mary sat talking. Mary did not want to be alone with him in the house, she would be awful uneasy to be inside with him.

As they sat there talking Mary noticed several bags of concrete mix stacked beneath the bay window. She started to ask him about them but decided against it, but she wondered what he was going to do with all that concrete. Mary listened very closely to what Jay had to say about Linda's disappearance, she was trying very hard to find something in his conversation that would tell her what she wanted to know. She got very nervous and excused herself to go home. She told Bob how uneasy she was when she was near Jay. She told Bob," I know Linda is nearby I can feel her."

"Do you think Jay has something to do with her disappearance? Bob asked.

"Yes, I do, but I don't know how or why, I do believe she is near."

The following weekend, Bob and Mary had planned to go visit Mary's parents that lived out of state. On Friday night around midnight Mary had to go to the bathroom. There was a full moon which made it seem like daylight outside. Mary didn't even turn the lights on it was so light. Mary could see Jay's house from the bathroom window. To her surprise and wonder she saw Jay outside his bay window digging in the flower bed. She thought to herself," what in the world is he doing out here at midnight digging in the flower bed?" She slipped back in bed but could not go to sleep just wondering what Jay was doing.

The next morning on their trip to see her parents, Mary told Bob about Jay digging in the flower bed at midnight. They both thought it was very strange and could not get it off their mind. When they returned home Sunday afternoon they discovered that Jay had built a fish pond and that was what he was digging that Friday night. He had dug that pond and lined it with concrete. He put a plastic liner inside the pool and filled it with water. There were gold fish in the pond.

After Bob and Mary saw the goldfish pond Mary said to Bob," I know where Linda is now Bob."

"Where do you think she may be?" Bob asked his wife.

"Bob, don't say anything to anyone, but I think she may be beneath the goldfish pond."

"Oh, no he wouldn't do something like that, would he? That is just too cruel I can't believe Jay would do it."

"Bob, I know that's where she is. He buried her there while we were gone. I just have a strong feeling about this Bob."

As time went on Jay hired a housekeeper that filled in as a babysitter. Mary and the housekeeper got acquainted and visited regularly, having coffee and doughnuts each morning. Their conversation would always turn to Linda and her disappearance. Mary would not tell the housekeeper what she thought about Linda and where she was.

Linda had only been gone two weeks when Bob and Mary were invited to a house party at the home of Mr. Kerry the local jewelry store owner. The conversation came around to the disappearance of Linda. Mr. Kerry said," oh, by the way, Dr. Jay brought all of Linda's jewelry in and sold it to me." He had taken all her clothes to the Clothes Closet and sold them.

After six months the doctor's dental business began to go downhill, he was losing his business.

He had to lay off his housekeeper and let Linda's parents keep the children. He kept Jane to the end. He sold everything in the house that he possibly could, he then moved in to a shabby apartment with Jane. He finally closed his dental business and him and Jane moved to another state.

The town was saddened and disappointed at his behavior.

The house stayed empty for over a year. It had a big

FOR SALE sign in the front yard. The middle of July a very young couple that had only been married a very short time bought the house and moved in. Ina and Greg Cannon were Mary and Bob's new neighbors.

Mary and Bob welcomed their new neighbors to the neighborhood. Mary and Ina became close friends with a chit chat across the back fence each morning. It was like old times to Mary when she and Linda would talk across the fence. They were good friends and best of neighbors.

A short time past and Mary became more acquainted with Ina, she began to tell her little things about Linda, what a nice person she was what a good friend she was. She also told her what a nice looking man Dr. Jay was and about him being a dentist and Linda was an RN at the hospital. She told her about all the good things that Linda did. How she liked to paint and the beautiful paintings that hung on their walls. Mary never mentioned the disappearance of Linda. She wanted to get to know her better before she would tell her such an awful gruesome story of the people that lived in the house before her.

Mary and Ina soon became as close as Mary and Linda were. The town and the neighborhood had slowly forgotten about the Newsom's and the ordeal with the Linda.

Mary soon told Ina about Jay killing his wife. She told her just a little at a time to keep from getting her scared to live in the house .Ina began to get inquisitive and would ask Mary different things about the disappearance of Linda. How did the doctor kill her and where was she buried. Mary told her about her feelings and the closeness she felt for Linda. Mary said," I can still feel her presence here. I know she's on this place somewhere."

"Where do you think she might be?" Ina asked Mary.

Mary answered her with sadness and grief in her voice. "Ina, I believe she is underneath the goldfish pond, I'm not sure but that's where I think she is."

When Greg came in from work that afternoon the

first thing Ina did was to tell Greg what Mary and she had talked about all afternoon. She told him Mary thought Linda was under the goldfish pond. Great could not believe his ears when he heard the awful story of what the doctor did to his wife.

That night, neither one of them could sleep just talked and thought about if it was true what Mary had told. It bared on their mind so hard for two weeks that finally Greg told Ina," honey, I can't stand this any longer just wondering if that lady is under that goldfish pond are not. I had rather dig it up and make sure than to just do nothing and wonder for all our lives if she would be underneath the pond."

The next morning Greg called a man he knew that had a backhoe and asked him if he would come over and dig his goldfish pond up. "I will be glad to dig it up for you Greg." The man replied.

"What time can you be here?" Greg asked.

"I'll be there first thing in the morning." The man answered.

"That will be fine I'll be here waiting for you, and

thank you very much." Greg said. With that said he hung the phone up and told Ina what the man said. She was glad that they would be relieved with the fact of knowing if she was or if she wasn't underneath the goldfish pond. They both slept sound that night. They had worried and wondered so long about what Mary told and now they were finally going to find out for sure.

Next morning they were up bright and early with a pot of hot coffee made and invited Mary over. When Mary walked past the goldfish pond she said," Good morning Linda, I know you're down there."

Greg and Ina were always glad to see Mary come for a visit. This morning was especially good. Greg began to tell Mary about their plans to dig the goldfish pond up. Mary suddenly got a deep sick feeling in her stomach and excuse to herself to go home. She had to pass by Linda one more time and tell her how much she missed her.

Mary then went to her house and waited for the man to come with the backhoe. When the man arrived Mary went to the fence and watched him as he began to dig the goldfish pond and all the concrete. When he had removed the concrete there he saw a black plastic bag. The man looked at Greg and motioned for him to get the bag. As he pulled the bag from the ground and arm fell out, then another bag with her head, the blond hair was all matted and some of it was hanging from the bag.

The entire neighborhood gathered close to the scene as possible and watched as each bag was removed. When the last bag was pulled from the ground the other arm failed to the ground.

Mary was watching as the arm fell to the ground. Mary fell to the ground also, she had fainted. She had found her dear friend and now she could rest and Linda could rest in peace.

Greg immediately went inside and called the police. They rushed to the scene and to their surprise they found what Mary had told them was true. It was a sad day for Mary and the McCorys now that the mystery of what happened to Linda was over.

Dr. Jay had opened a new dental clinic in a little town near Memphis, Tennessee and was doing very well.

While he was working on the patient with his white coat on and looked so professional, two heavily armed policemen came barging in and asked if he was Jacob Newsom. When he looked up he answered them," yes I am, what may I do for you nice gentlemen?" They hurriedly spun him around and handcuffed him then swiftly marched him outside to a waiting patrol car.

"What is going on? What is this all about?" Jay asked the policemen.

"It's all about you. You are a suspect in the murder of your wife." One of the policemen answered.

They put him in the back seat of the patrol car and quickly sped off. They didn't give him time to tell Jane goodbye or his patient. They transported him back to where he had committed the crime and locked him in jail there. He waited in jail for more than six months before his trial date.

The day of his trial the court room was full with people that were his past patients, his neighbors and many curious onlookers. Everyone wanted to see the man that so cruelly killed his precious wife.

No one was surprised when Jacob Newsom was accused of killing his wife and dismembering her body and burying it beneath their goldfish pond. The jury found him guilty of first-degree murder of his wife Linda Newsom. He was sentenced to life in prison without any possibility of parole.

To this day Jacob Newsom is sitting behind the prison walls at Perchman, Mississippi.

Since his confinement Dr. Jay has not had any messages from anyone or had any visits from anyone, not even his family. It looks as though everyone in the world had forgotten him. Even Jane soon forgot about him.

Was Dr. Jay so in love with Jane that he would kill his wife and lose his family, business and all the friends he had, just for the love of Jane. Was Jacob Newsom just an evil hardhearted, handsome individual that cared nothing for anyone except himself?

Some people think he will burn in hell. What do you think?

Gone Fishing

THE SWEET SMELL of honeysuckle filled the air as the gentle breeze nudged the leaves of the tall cypress trees that line the bank of the huge lake. The sun glistened brightly on the slowly rippling water, as the two men watched as their bright red bobbers were rising up and down with the gentle waves. Near the men, attached firmly to the bank, was a stringer with half a dozen fairly large bream destined to be tonight's supper. The men watched their lines closely for the next catch to pull their bobbers down signaling another fight with a fish that would be cleaned, battered and fried, making a feast enjoyed in the South for generations.

Although quite for now the two had already discussed the problems of the world their opinions of such and how they would resolve them. The upcoming elections, the high cost of gasoline, the rising crime rate and the increasing number of incoming aliens which they referred to as Mexecons had all been hashed out and solved by these two simple men.

The older of the two removed his cap revealing a head full of snow white hair that blew softly in the breeze. He wiped at the light shimmering sweat that had moistened his weather-beaten brow. His steely blue eyes never left the floating bobber as he waited patiently and with anticipation for another lake fish to put on the stringer.

The younger fishermen fidgeted slightly as he tried to ease some of the stiffness the hours of sitting in the same position had caused. Although his bare head had no white hair his brilliantly blue eyes matched those of the older man and there was little doubt that he shared many of the traits of his father.

He looked out across the wide expanse of the lake admiring the wondrous beauty before him, the deep blue water reflecting the cloudless Tennessee sky. High above an eagle floated silently a long looking for his own meal to swoop down and harvest from the waters below. Off to his left he could see one of the many ducks that lived on the lake splashing along the shoreline and being followed by five young ducklings that ducked their heads in and out of the water as if mystified by the New World they had entered not long ago. He could hear the sounds of the summertime crickets as they signaled for mates and the mingled chirping of a multitude of birds in the trees behind them and the rapid tapping of a woodpecker far off in the distance.

He thought about the tragic formation of this lake that had happened so long ago, the huge earth quake that rocked this once flat land and changed it into a place of deep hollows and high ridges. Shaking and rumbling the landscape had changed and the great

Lake had been filled with water from the Mississippi River in a three day transformation that made it flow backward until the lake was full and the River resumed its flow to the South. He tried to imagine what the Indians who had lived here at that time must have thought as the earth moved, split and shook beneath their feet, the fear and terror they must have endured as entire villages were wiped out and lost forever. "But that was then and this is now", he thought and his mind and eyes returned to the natural beauty of his surroundings. When they plan to go fishing the older man always wanted to get up early in the morning, around daybreak and get started on the way to the lake. It was a beautiful morning, the little breeze that was blowing, was crisp and there was not a cloud in the sky. The water in the lake was smooth as glass except for the little ripples around the bank. "This is going to be a great day for fishing", both of them thought, as they began to make their hooks with the earthworms they had dug the day before.

Minutes passed as the two sat alone on the bank

and then the younger man turned to his father and said, "You know, dad, I have always wondered if you thought mom was the best fish Cooker in the world. You are always saying how good the fish are when she fries them. I heard you tell her one time that the fish she fried was the best in the world. Is that true dad?"

Still watching his bobber, the old man said, "Yes, son, she is the best cook I ever saw." At that moment his bobber went under and he started pulling in a big Bream. "Look at this one, Son, it's the biggest one we've caught so for."

"Yes, Sir, it's the first one we've caught", the son said laughingly.

As the sun was beginning to sink into the West, and the water in the lake was still calm and warm, he pulled off his hat and fanned himself for a while thinking it was so nice and peaceful.

The dad looked at his son, thinking it was about time to load up and start toward Union City, but his son was so absorbed in the little ducks and their surroundings, he didn't want to disturb him. As he placed his ragged cap back on his head, he looked across the lake, over to his left was what he thought was a big cotton sack floating ever so slowly. "Jeff, look at that sack, what do you make of that?"

"I don't know dad. Is that a hand hanging out of it? "Jeff asked. "I don't think so," he chuckled, "but guess it could be, we can tell in a minute when it floats closer to us."

They waited for it to come closer but it seemed to have stopped still and wouldn't move. They waited and watched for it to move with the small waves but it just stayed where it was. It was very apparent that it had snagged on one of the hundreds of cypress knees that jutted up out of the water around the bank. "Jeff, I'm going to try to cast out there and snagged it and maybe I can drag it in, and if it is a hand, I'm going to run like hell," the older man laughed. His experienced eyes measured the distance to the floating bag, and he arched back his arm and rod and threw it in its direction. His sharp hook landed directly atop the bag and he began to reel in the line slowly, but his hook only slid across the top and then landed back in the water with a small plop. "Dang," he said, "I'll try again", and he flung his gear toward the mysterious bag again. It landed solid on it and this time the hook caught. In a slow practiced manner he began to pull the bag toward them. As it inched toward them it left the small trickle as it cut through the breeze blown waves.

Jeff watched anxiously as it slowly came toward them. As it got closer he said, "Well Pop, that ain't no hand, but I am not sure just what it is."

"We'll find out in a minute." the older man said.

Suddenly a gruff voice behind them said, "Well, what the heck do you think you're doing old man?"

Jeff and his dad did look back and there behind them stood one really large man, but what immediately caught their eyes was the enormous pistol he held pointed toward them.

"Maybe you should just get your fish and get out here", he said never taking the gun off of them.

Jeff, looking at the gunman, thought it strange the

man was in a sheriff's uniform and he slowly sized him up. The deputy was well over 6 feet tall and his shoulders were broad and wide but despite his size there was no fat on his obviously strong and sculptured body. He was wearing a khaki uniform, as they all did. The man's badge was gold and he had Captain' bars on his lapels. "No small time deputy here", he thought. "This guy is a big dog for sure."

The huge blue-steel automatic pistol was pointed at them, steadily and did not waiver. Off behind the man he saw a black unmarked Crown Vic cruiser parked in the trees beside his dad old pickup.

He turned to his father and saw pure anger in his blue eyes as he glared at the deputy. "All heck", he thought, "this could surely turned ugly".

"Hey, Pop, maybe we should just go," he said.

"Yes, we should", the older man said and started reeling in his line attached to the bag.

"Just leave that alone and be on your way", the burly deputy said.

"Alright," the older man said as he dropped his rod

and started gathering up his thermos jug and tackle box.

Jeff started packing up his gear and leaned over the bank. Retrieve the stringer full of fish they had caught. As he pulled the stringer from the water, one of the larger Bream flopped and hit the water hard.

The deputy, hearing the splash, looked over sharply. The next sound he heard was the distinct mechanical sound of a revolver being cocked as he felt the cold steel of the barrel pushing into his ear. In a strong voice the older man said," "now big boy, if you don't want your brains blown out of the other side of your head, you just hand that little cap Pistol of yours over to my boy there, real slow".

Jeff looked over his shoulder and could not believe his eyes. In a moment of distraction of a flopping fish, his dad had pulled a 38 from his waist band and now had it firmly pressed against the big deputy's head, and although a foot taller than the older man, he was obviously shaken and had lowered the weapon he had brandished before. Jeff quickly rose and took the huge automatic from the cop noticing now the big man was shaking and had a startled look in his once steady eyes. Then, in a stammering voice, he heard him say "You are making a big mistake, old man".

"The only mistake here," his father answered," is you pulling a gun on me and my son. I don't take that lightly and sure don't like being threatened and I don't leave my rod and reel behind for nothing. Now suppose you tell me why you are here and just what this is all about".

At that very moment another deputy drove up and rushed from the marked vehicle he was driving, to where the big bad Sheriff was. "Come on, Sheriff, we are needed down the highway". A meadow was between the lake and the highway. Cows were grazing on the fresh green spring grass. The cows raised their heads as a police car came roaring down the highway with the siren going full blast. The older man dropped the pistol he was holding on the Sheriff, down to his side. Thinking all this time, "What in the world was going on." The two deputies ran to their cars, thinking there must be an emergency down the highway. "Hey, Sheriff, wait, here is your gun", the son yelled as he ran to the Sheriff with his pistol. "Thanks", the Sheriff said, and away the Sheriff went leaving a fog of dust behind.

"Wonder what that's all about" the dad asked.

"I don't know but he scared the living daylights out of me. Something bad must have happened down the highway", the son said. They were not about to let that Sheriff scare them away.

The older man picked up his rod and reel and cast it toward the bag. His hook snagged the bag but it slipped off. He cast it one more time and this time it snagged the bag tight. He pulled it in. As they got it to the bank and began to open the bag, the older man said, "Let's see what might be in this thing now." The bag held nothing but old life jackets, floats, lines, hooks and all kind of fishing equipment. "Someone must have thrown this away because it is no good, go throw it in that trash barrel over there by that tree", the dad said to his son.

Over in the West small thunderheads were gathering in the clear blue sky. They were looking at the formation of the clouds and trying to make out an object from them. There was so much beauty around as they scanned the lake up and down the bank and across the lake. There were small dark spots in the late and near the bank on the other side of the lake, it was fisherman in their boats trying to catch that big bass they had always dreamed of.

"Let's go home now, son, you're ma will be worried about us if we are gone too long. It's getting late now so let's head back to Union City. "

"Okay, dad", Jeff answered. They started gathering their fishing gear together when a stranger came up and spoke to them. "Had any luck today?" The stranger asked, looking at the long string of bream, Jeff, was pulling from the lake, "just a little bit, " the older man said.

"I heard there was a bank robbery down at Troy, have you heard anything about it?" The stranger asked.

"No, but the Sheriff was out here acting smart with

us about an old cotton sack full of junk fishing gear that was hung on a snag out in the lake. He must've thought that was the money and we were the robbers". This silver haired man answered, "We must get started we have a fur piece to go."

The sky was turning a mulky gray over in the west the clouds were beginning to get thicker. They could see a small streak of lightning and hear the faraway rumble of thunder. The wind started to blow and made ripples on the water. They knew it was going to rain so they hurriedly picked up their belongings and started walking down the path toward the truck, when a mighty gust of wind blew and it made a whirlwind with the dust in front of them.

As they slowly inched the truck up to the main highway, the driver looked both ways, maybe a quarter of a mile up the highway to their right, they saw a lot of blue flashing lights from police cars that was near the spillway.

"Wonder what that is up there, they must've found

the bank Robbers, I would go up there, but I don't want to get in all that traffic." The dad said.

"Oh!, I bet it is the robbers, " the son said. They turn left and started towards Union City. When they got to Troy there was a road block, traffic was backed up just waiting. As the two fishermen eased their pick-up to where the cops were standing, they were checking driver's licenses.

The older man asked, "What's all the commotion about?"

The policeman replied in a very calm voice, "We had a bank to get robbed this morning, but we just heard on the radio that they caught him at Reelfoot Lake." With that said, he motioned the older man to go on.

"Man, what a day this is been, but we got a mess of the fish and that's what we came after." The dad said. As they arrived at the city limits of Union City. "I'm tired and still have these fish to clean tonight,"

They drove across town to their home on Cloys Road.

The son said, "Thanks, Dad, I enjoyed fishing and all the commotion we have seen today. Maybe we can do this again soon, I like to fish at Reelfoot Lake."

The dad, smiled at his tired son and said, "We will go back soon, son". With a handshake and a hug, they both walked inside the house and began to tell Ma about their day of fishing and all the commotion that went on at Reelfoot Lake.

Betty Ruth Burden Wood was born and raised in Union City, Tennessee. She is the daughter of the late John Elvie and Lucy Turner Burden. She is the youngest and only living child of eight siblings; James, Charles, Madge, Dorothy, Redge, Glover, and Bobby.

Betty is the mother of four wonderful children, Judy Kaye Smith of Star City, Arkansas, Doug Dane of Eugene, Oregon, Farrah Ann Campbell of Trenton, Tennessee and Donna Rushin Newman of Star City, Arkansas.

I was encouraged to write a small book of short stories after I had written a book of my early life in Tennessee. My friends and family all encouraged me to keep writing.

I would like to thank my husband, Floyd and my children, along with a very special stepson, Donald Rushing and wife, Kathy, for making this dream of mine come true.